Megan Owlet

WRITTEN AND ILLUSTRATED BY
BETH ANNE MARESCA

Sky Pony Press
New York

Sky Pony Press books may be purchased in bulk at special discounts for sales promotion, corporate gifts, fund-raising, or educational purposes. Special editions can also be created to specifications. For details, contact the Special Sales Department, Sky Pony Press, 307 West 36th Street, 11th Floor, New York, NY 10018 or info@skyhorsepublishing.com.

Sky Pony® is a registered trademark of Skyhorse Publishing, Inc.®, a Delaware corporation.

Visit our website at www.skyponypress.com.

10 9 8 7 6 5 4 3 2 1

Manufactured in China, December 2014
This product conforms to CPSIA 2008

Library of Congress Cataloging-in-Publication Data

Maresca, Beth Anne, author, illustrator.
Megan Owlet / Beth Anne Maresca.
pages cm
Summary: Tired of just supporting her big brothers in their activities, Megan Owlet tries to find something of her own to do and when she decides dancing is right for her, her brothers are there to help her succeed.
ISBN 978-1-63220-404-2 (hardback)
[1. Brothers and sisters—Fiction. 2. Individuality—Fiction. 3. Determination (Personality trait)—Fiction. 4. Dance—Fiction. 5. Owls—Fiction.] I. Title.
PZ7.1.M37Meg 2015
[E]—dc23
2014033685

Cover design by Sarah Brody
Cover illustration credit Beth Anne Maresca

Ebook ISBN: 978-1-63220-824-8

Megan Owlet hid deep under the covers. It was going to be another busy Saturday spent following her three big brothers to all of their activities. But Megan didn't want to go.

"Megan! Time to go!" Andrew called.

"C'mon, Megan!" called Luke.

"Megan, I can see your feathers!" said Ian.

Megan slowly crawled out of bed and followed the boys out the door.

Usually, Megan loved being there for her brothers. She was the loudest clapper, the most enthusiastic cheerer, and was extra great at rousing the crowd.

"You can do it!" she yelled. "Go, Owls, go!"

But today, Megan didn't feel like cheering.

She felt like fidgeting,
climbing, and pouting instead.

"What has gotten into you?" her mother asked.
"I'm bored," Megan said. "I want an activity, too!"
"Did you have something special in mind?" asked her mother.

Megan didn't really know what she wanted to do. But her brothers had lots of ideas.

"Megan, you should try basketball. You'll love it!" Andrew said.

"Hyyyaaaahhhh! Try karate!" Luke said.

"Come play violin with me," Ian said. "We can play a duet."

Megan wasn't sure which activity to choose. So she tried them all.

When Megan dribbled the basketball, the hoop was higher than she remembered and the ball was just too bouncy!

At karate, Megan kept tripping on the clothes, and she really wished they were pink.

Finally, when Megan tried the violin, the bow got tangled in her pigtails. Ouch! None of these activities were right for her.

Megan needed a new plan.

"Huddle up!" she said to her animal friends. But after a long thinking session, Megan was left uninspired. And it was time to pick up the boys, again.

On the way, Megan saw something
that made her feathers ruffle. She
let out a loud SCREECH
and pointed across the road.
"Is this something you'd like to
try?" her mother asked.
"Oh, I know it is!" said Megan.

That night Megan went to bed . . .

and dreamed of all the things she would do in dance class.

But when she arrived the next day, Megan's tummy wobbled with worry.

It was hard to follow along.
She went up when she was supposed
to go down. She went down when the
class spun.
She even bumped into her ballet
teacher, twice!

At the end of class, the teacher announced that they
would all be dancing in the spring recital!

Owl Theater
presents a
Spring Recital

Please join us
Friday May 14th

Everyone laughed and cheered!
Everyone, but Megan.

Megan's brothers were there watching and knew just what to do.

"I can teach you to jump," Andrew said.

"I can help you balance and kick," Luke said.

"And I can help you move to the beat," Ian said.

Megan loved this plan!

Twirl. Pose. 1-2-3.

Jump. Kick. 1-2-3.

Spin. Leap. 1-2-3.

It was hard work, but after weeks of preparation, Megan was ready for the recital.

Before the show, Megan peeked out at the audience.
Her tummy had that funny feeling again.

When the curtain opened, everyone began to dance.

Everyone, but Megan.

Her feet felt stuck, and her wings were so heavy.

Megan's beak quivered.

But Megan's brothers were there, watching.
"Huddle up!" Andrew whispered. "We need a plan."

Megan was about to give up, when she heard . . . cheering. "You can do it!" the boys yelled.

Megan smiled, feeling a little braver.
She took a deep breath and began to
move to the music.

The boys clapped louder.
"Bravo!" she heard them say.
And with that, Megan's worries floated away.

She suddenly felt light as a feather!
Megan twirled and kicked and soared across the stage!

Best of all, having her family there made Megan feel as if she could do anything!

For Olenka and Christina
—C.S.

The Silk Princess

Charles Santore

Random House ⌂ New York

The legend of the secret thread begins five thousand years ago in China, the ancient Middle Kingdom. The Emperor Huang-Ti and his noble Empress, Lei-Tsu, had two sons, whom the Emperor doted upon.

He also had a young daughter, the princess Hsi-Ling Chi, whom he hardly noticed.

The Great Emperor, descended from the sons of heaven, was a grand figure. Regal in his bearing, he reigned in splendor. Although his riches could afford him any pleasure, he was greatly displeased with his royal garments and had spent years searching for fabric worthy of his nobility. His quest had been unsuccessful, until one fine day, in a pleasant corner of the royal gardens, the search came to an end.

On this fine afternoon, the Empress and Princess Hsi-Ling Chi were enjoying the royal gardens. The Empress was sitting in the shade of a mulberry tree, enjoying her afternoon tea. She watched her daughter playing among the spring flowers and did not notice when a cream-colored cocoon fell from the tree above her and landed in her teacup. The little princess, however, did.

Hsi-Ling Chi peered into the teacup and was astonished to see the cocoon unraveling in the hot tea, forming a long, delicate thread.

"Oh, Mother, look. It's as fine as your hair!" she cried, holding up one end of the shimmering thread. The Empress smiled and asked, "Shall we see how long it is?"

"Yes!" Hsi-Ling Chi replied, delighted at her mother's proposal. "I know," she shouted. "I will tie this end of the thread around my waist, and you, Mother, will hold the cocoon. I shall walk away from you, and we shall see how long this fine thread is. I will go to the end of the gardens, should the thread reach that far!" The Empress agreed, for she never imagined the cocoon would unravel to the end of the royal gardens.

Hsi-Ling Chi, anxious to begin the game, kissed her mother goodbye, bowed, and started on her way. Attached to the thread, the little princess glided away from her mother, like a kite on a gentle breeze.

She walked past rock formations representing the Holy Mountains, beside glistening pools, and continued on, looking back from time to time to see her mother getting smaller and smaller in the distance. Princess Hsi-Ling Chi had never been away from her mother before, yet she did not hesitate.

"I am not afraid at all! This must be a magical thread!" she thought as she walked along.

After a while, feeling a little sleepy, Hsi-Ling Chi yawned and stretched out on the cool grass in the shade of an ancient tree and fell into a deep sleep.

When she awoke, the little princess looked around in wonder. Unfamiliar trees and plants of every description lined her way. She passed among camellias, magnolias, and beautiful, fragrant flowers.

She was so taken with the lovely blossoms that she nearly walked right into an enormous spider's web that stretched across her path. "Watch where you're going! Are you trying to destroy my web?" Startled, Hsi-Ling Chi found herself face to face with an angry, glaring spider. Before she could utter a word, the spider hissed again, "This is *my* lair! Find your own place to spin your flimsy web!"

The frightened little princess apologized. Bowing deeply, she slowly backed away, then found a safer path through the flowers.

Ahead towered the palace entrance, and still the thread had not reached its end.

Hsi-Ling Chi kept going, and soon she passed out of the royal gardens and through the great gates of the palace itself.

All the guards at the entrance bowed as the princess walked past them. "I am outside!" she shouted. "I'm outside of the royal palace! Even Mother has never been this far!" Hsi-Ling Chi looked around in amazement. In the distance, she saw the Holy Mountains rising into the clouds.

As she walked along the wide road leading away from the palace, from time to time the little princess would touch the shiny thread that tied her to her mother.

"This is truly an adventure," she thought to herself. "I have heard wondrous stories at court about the world beyond the palace. Some say there is even a terrible dragon that sleeps under the bridge leading to the Holy Mountains. It is said that to cross the bridge, one must be careful not to wake him, for he can hear the faintest footfall. I can be very quiet," the little princess said to herself, "and I would so love to see a dragon."

Gradually, the road began to rise, at first gently and then steeply as it wound higher into the mountains. Hsi-Ling Chi came to a bridge spanning a deep gorge. "This must be where the dragon sleeps," she thought.

It was so silent, only the sound of the wind could be heard. The princess was no longer sure she wanted to see a dragon, but still she was determined to cross the bridge.

Carefully, the princess removed her shoes, closed her eyes, and dashed barefoot onto the bridge, with the long, shiny thread stretching out behind her.

In her haste, the little princess stumbled and dropped one of her wooden shoes onto the bridge. It landed with a *crack*. The sound echoed off the rocks and filled the gorge. Suddenly she heard a mighty roar, and a huge dragon emerged right behind her!

Hsi-Ling Chi scooped up her shoe and ran for her life. The beast sprang, its jaws snapping to devour her.

But the dragon's huge claws tripped over the shiny thread, sending the monster hurtling into the gorge and onto the rocks below.

The terrified princess reached the other side and kept running until the bridge was far behind her.

He crept down the stairs.

CRASH

There was Grandpa.

12

Sam broke three eggs into a bowl and stirred. Grandpa added milk.

Uh-oh. In the bowl, not on the table, Gramps.

Grandpa grabbed chocolate sprinkles. He put them on the eggs.

Is that pepper?

Hee-hee

15

Sam and Grandpa
made toast . . .

. . . with honey.

Sam crawled onto Grandpa's lap.
They ate chocolate eggs and toast.

Yum!

16

Suddenly the stairs creaked!

Uh-oh.

Mama came in.

WHAT A MESS!

I told you NO cooking, Sam! You BAD BOY!

17

Mama marched Sam upstairs.

Tomorrow you will clean that mess, you bad boy.

In the dark, Sam explained.

Grandpa was making a mess and asked me to help, Mama.

So Mama kissed Sam good night.

We'll both clean the kitchen tomorrow. Sleep tight, Sammy. My good boy.

18

When Mama left, Grandpa tiptoed in.

Thank you for helping, Sam. What a good boy!

LEAVES

Wind scuttled the leaves in circles.
On the way to school, Sam and Olive
chased them. They rolled around in
them and kicked them high.

They gave leaf bouquets to their teacher, Mrs. Crow.

Thank you, children.

Some got a little squashed.

Today is leaf day.

Mrs. Crow handed out leaf outlines.
Latoya's paw shot up.

May we have a leaf coloring contest?

20

21

Sam got up. He slipped on a crayon.

Everyone laughed again, except Latoya.

Sam did it again.

So did Olive.

You BOTH go cool off in the paint corner!

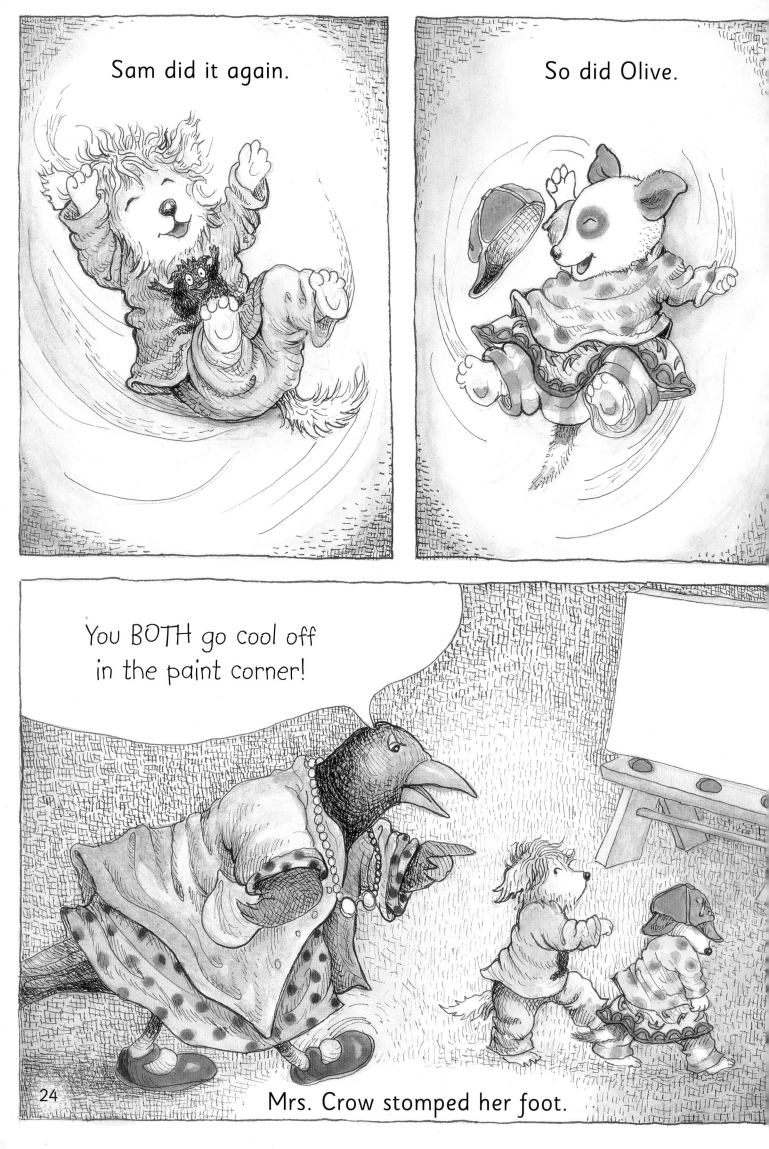

Mrs. Crow stomped her foot.

Olive picked up a paintbrush.

SOON PAINT WAS FLYING.

Sam slipped out from behind the curtain. No one saw.

He pulled on his boots and slicker.

He ran outside. No one saw.

28

He grabbed branches.

He waved them and stomped on them.

He piled them into a wild heap.

No one saw.

Mama noticed Sam was gone.

30

Mama, Papa, Grandma, and Grandpa
peered inside. There sat Sam.

31

I built a big nest for Birdie. He fell out of a tree.
I saw from the window.

Good Boy!

Peep, peep!

32